Somebody's Sleeping In My Bed

Somebody's Sleeping In My Bed

▼

A Hot Fiction Novel

Rosiland Cole- Crossland

iUniverse, Inc.
New York Lincoln Shanghai

Somebody's Sleeping In My Bed
A Hot Fiction Novel

All Rights Reserved © 2003 by Rosiland Crossland

No part of this book may be reproduced or transmitted in any form or by any means, graphic, electronic, or mechanical, including photocopying, recording, taping, or by any information storage retrieval system, without the written permission of the publisher.

iUniverse, Inc.

For information address:
iUniverse, Inc.
2021 Pine Lake Road, Suite 100
Lincoln, NE 68512
www.iuniverse.com

This is a work of fiction. Names, characters, incidents and places are the products of the author's imagination.
First Edition

ISBN: 0-595-30216-5

Printed in the United States of America

In Memory of:

Lelia Mathews

Carrie Miller

J.C. miller

Eddie Mae Cole

Dedicated to:

Adaisha Crossland

Alexis Crossland

Amber Crossland

Chassidy Grimes

Xaivier Woods

Acknowledgements

Thanks to: God almighty. This wouldn't have been possible without him. My husband, Andre Crossland for supporting my writing career. My Children, Adaisha, Alexis, and Amber. My mom, Shirley Cole, for helping me grow spiritually throughout the years. My dad, Babe Cole, for believing in me and supporting me. My friend, Cassandra Berry, for encouraging me to hurry up and get this book out on the market. My sisters Lynn, Michelle, and Brittany for being there and lending me a listening ear. My brothers Babe and Bernard. The author, Darren Colemen, for providing me with some pertinent information about the book market. My friends, Jenice Jacobson and Natasha Briscoe. St. Jude for caring for my child while I completed this book. Angelicare Flying Start Child Care Center. I would also like to thank Fullview Missionary Baptist Church for keeping my family in their prayers. Brenda Carr Mckinney for helping me also.

Thanks For Supporting My Talents
—Rosiland Cole- Crossland

A Hot Pocket Novel

Summary

Star James knew she had a perfect marriage. She married the man of her dreams. They had a nice home. She was living happily ever after. Her husband had more money than anyone could ever dream of having; but, their marriage is put to the test. Star's husband starts acting strange. She's sure it is related to his career. Is it related to his career, or is he involved in something else? One of the characters in this book experience an ordeal that is so dramatic, You will think it is happening right before your eyes. This book is for anyone that has been scorned before. It also shows you the consequences of trying to establish a perfect relationship. Find out what the consequences are if you're thinking about putting your marriage or relationship to the test. You might end up creating a test that's too hard for you to pass. One of the characters in this book had to find out the hard way.

Chapter 1

My name is Star James, and I am a successful, thirty year old, African American, stay at home wife. I have long, black hair and honey,colored eyes. My skin is the color of cocoa, but I am not a Jet magazine swim suit beauty or anything. You see I am a plus size woman. I am 5 feet and ten inches tall, and I currently weigh two hundred pounds even; but, I wear my size twenty two with plenty of poise and passion. Let me explain myself. The years have been extremely kind to me. I married the man of my dreams.

His name is Keith "too tall" James. We met in high school, and we have been in love every since. We married one year after graduating from high school. Keith went to college on a basketball scholarship. He went pro right after college. Keith is the star player for the Chicago Spurs. Keith has made a lot of money in his lifetime. Some people work until old age, and they still don't come close to the money that pro athletes make. Keith is a sexy looking brother. People compare him to Michael Jordan, but Keith is a lot lighter. I always dreamed of becoming a teacher, but my college plans went down the drain. Keith said that he would never marry a career woman. He wanted someone to cook hot meals and do the laundry. You might call me a fool; but, if you lived in my world for one day you would give up your career too.

Keith is pretty easy to get along with. Keith only requires that I cook three hot meals a day. He also likes for me to iron all his casual attire in advance. He bought me a riding lawn mower, because he hates an uncut yard. We live in an upscale Chicago neighborhood, so I can understand the yard thing. I suggested hiring a yard man once, but Keith said it was a waste of money. I am the only woman in the neighborhood that does her own yard.

Keith and I spent a lot of time together during his college days. Our time grew shorter and shorter after Keith signed with the Chicago Spurs. We see each other about two weeks out of every month now . Keith is always traveling, and when he's in town he's working out. Keith bought me a membership to the gym last month. He said that I needed something to occupy my time. I am going to start using my membership, because I could use some fresh air every now and then.

Chapter 2

If you subtract a few small irregularities, Keith and I are the picture of a perfect marriage. People always say that every marriage has its flaws, but I disagree. Keith and I are like a fairy tale couple. We are trying to add a baby to the family, but we have been unsuccessful each time. In the meantime I am going to have fun trying. Keith is a semi romantic man. Let me explain myself. Keith loves fore play, role play, and more fore play, and then it's two whole minutes of semi incredible sex. Yes, two minutes and that's all.

Keith likes to pretend a lot before we engage in romance. Sometimes he pretends as if he's Charlie and I am one of the angels. We have an intercom system in our house, and Keith gets on it and gives me commands. We were adding some spice to our sex life one night, and I accidentally handcuffed Keith to the bed and lost the key. The police were called to our home, and Keith was real embarrassed. I know it sounds crazy, but it's fun.

We have been doing all this role playing and fore playing, and I am still without child. The doctors have performed numerous tests on both of us, and they have determined that I have Endometriosis. This is a condition that causes a woman's uterus to develop outside of the pelvic area. The doctor's said that my condition could become severe over a period of time. If that happens I will be forced to have a hysterectomy. Keith hates to discuss my female problems. He has always dreamed of fatherhood. He said a little boy would be nice. They could play ball together, and a boy would carry on his name. I suggested adoption, but Keith wants to try a couple more times.

I have had eight surgeries to try and correct my problem, but so far I have encountered one disappointment after another. I stay up to wee hours in the night reading articles and books in hopes that I will find a doctor that can correct my problem. My neighbor went to a doctor that specializes in the female body. She paid a fortune to have an Invitro Fertilization, and the treatment worked the first time. She finally got pregnant. The doctor is located in Europe, and my neighbor spoke highly of him. I might consider going to my neighbor's doctor. I have tried everything else. Infertility becomes very depressing for me sometimes. I have even thought about trying to find a surrogate mother. I was raised by my grandmother, and she said that women should submit to their husbands. Sometimes I feel as if I am not submitting to Keith. He wants a baby, and I can't give it to him.

Chapter 3

I was very lonesome when Keith was away from home. I finally decided to use my membership at the gym . I started working out daily at The Windy City Gym. The gym was about 5 miles from our estate. I met a lady at the gym who had just moved into the neighborhood. Her name was Belinda Jenkins. She had moved in to an upscale apartment high-rise directly across the street. Ms. Jenkins is like a mother figure. She is ten years older than me, and she gives pretty sound advice. I told her about my female problems, and she said that God doesn't put more on us than we can bear.

Ms. Jenkins and I talked at the gym on daily basis. She started sharing her problems with me. She told me about her two daughters, their names were Evelyn and Elizabeth. Evelyn is thirteen. She's a straight A student, and she is very respectful to her elders. Elizabeth is the total opposite. The saying says that you can take a person out of the ghetto, but you can't take the ghetto out of the person. They're talking about Elizabeth.

Elizabeth is a menace to our entire neighborhood. Her family moved to The Millennium Hills Estates after Mr. Jenkins died and left them a fortune. Elizabeth is a nineteen year old problem. She dresses like a whore, and she often walks through our upscale neighborhood looking like a cheap trick. The neighborhood men rave over Elizabeth. They treat her like some sick prize. I have often seen her flouncing around the neighborhood with married men while their wives were not present. Elizabeth wears a tattoo on her right arm. It's a tattoo with a black serpent on it. I haven't been fond of her since I saw that thing. Her tattoo symbolizes evilness.

Our neighborhood was drama free, and then Elizabeth came along. I was raised to believe that the devil was a red creature with horns and a pitch fork; but, the devil can be in the form of anything. He wears high heels and tight dresses too. He likes to break up marriages and destroy happy homes. He will find your weakness, and then he will reel you in. He will reel you in like a fish on a hook.

I have often seen Elizabeth giving my husband the eye, but it is not all about what occurs. It all about how you handle it. I have already talked to my husband about the Elizabeth problem, and he knows that I will hurt him if he ever goes near that woman. Keith and I are in love, and I know that he would never dream of someone as cheap as Elizabeth. We discussed Elizabeth at the dinner table tonight, and Keith said that she works the streets in other parts of Chicago. He kept on saying how it was a shame for her to waste her pretty body on sinful things.

I felt a little down in the dumps after talking to Keith, he has never called my body pretty. I started to feel like Keith and I were growing apart. He was so caught up in the team lately. It was like he didn't have time for me anymore. Our anniversary was yesterday. I fixed him a candlelight dinner; but, all he gave me was a ticket to an Ebony Arie concert that was in town. He only bought one ticket as if I wanted to go by myself. He could have at least bought two tickets. I could have asked Ms. Jenkins to go if he didn't want to.

Chapter 4

Today is January 4, 2003. I had to rush like crazy this morning, because I finally decided to try that doctor in Europe. I caught a 5:00 A.M. flight into Europe, and I arrived about ten hours later. Europe has one of the best female hospitals in the world. Keith and I are paying $50,000 out of our pockets to have another surgery to correct my uterus. The surgery will only take a couple of hours, and it will take my body about four weeks to recover from it. I was on the table in the operating room, and I can remember asking the surgeon when he was going to start performing surgery. He said that my surgery had been completed. Anesthesia does that to your mind. It puts you into a very deep sleep. I couldn't even remember checking myself into the hospital. I couldn't remember a thing.

I started going through a state of depression after the surgery, because I didn't hear from Keith at all. He didn't call me at all while I was in Europe. He didn't know if I was alive or dead. I tried calling the house, but the answering machine kept coming on. I decided that this would be my last and final surgery. I am not going to keep allowing the doctors to cut on me like some lab rat. I 've been through one surgery after another while Keith's body remains all flawless and untouched.

Keith is going to have to accept my body in the condition that it's in. We married for better or worse. Keith is going to have to get a grip on life and accept the fact that I can't have a baby. I am going to start treating my body like a holy temple, and I am not going to have anymore useless surgeries. Keith will get over it sooner or later.

Chapter 5

I arrived back in town this morning, and I am as sore as you can imagine. The doctor advised me to stay off of my feet for about four weeks. He said six would be even better. When I finally arrived home my house was a disaster. Keith had dirty dishes and beer cans everywhere. My carpet was all dirty, and worst of all my bedroom smelled rank. There was a very gross smell in my bedroom. Keith wasn't home, but he left the window raised up. I wasn't quite sure if Keith had been partying or what. The smell in my bedroom led me to believe that he might be somewhere sick.

My bedroom had a musty smell in it . It smelled like rotten onions or something. It took me hours to get that smell out of my bedroom. I had to run to the store and buy a huge air filter just to get that smell out of my bedroom. I started having some sharp pains in my stomach. I guess it's from cleaning so much, because I came home cleaning and trying to get that awful smell out of my house. I decided to get off my feet, so I jumped in bed and turned the television on the Young and Restless. My sheets were all dirty and dingy. I was so mad at Keith. It looked as if he hadn't cleaned up for days. I decided to check my caller i.d. box while I was watching the soaps. Ms. Jenkins' number was the first number on the list. I was a little puzzled, because her number was on the box at 12:01 A.M. on a Saturday night. Ms. Jenkins' didn't have any reason to call my house that night. She knew I was out of town.

I started thinking about the situation more and more, and something in my mind said that Elizabeth was probably the one that called my house. That low down, cheap, dirty slut. She could have easily looked across the street and picked up on the fact that I was gone, or she could have ran into my husband somewhere and threw herself all over him. I was so mad I couldn't even watch the Bold and the Beautiful.

I cut the television off, and I went to look for Ms. Jenkins' number. I decided to call Ms. Jenkins and get to the bottom of this matter. Ms. Jenkins answered the phone, and she said that everyone in her house was in bed by 11:00 P.M. Saturday night. "Wait a minute," she said. " Elizabeth was up way past midnight." Ms. Jenkins assured me that Elizabeth did not leave the house. Ms. Jenkins said it had to be some kind of mistake. I told Ms. Jenkins that I was sitting there looking at her number on the caller i.d. box. Ms. Jenkins said that she would talk to Elizabeth and get back in touch with me later. I didn't hear from Ms. Jenkins anymore. She even stopped working out at the gym with me.

Maybe it wasn't Elizabeth that called my house. It could have been Ms. Jenkins. She's really not that old. Ms. Jenkins is a very pretty woman. Maybe she has a thing for my husband or something. Keith talked so bad about Elizabeth at the dinner table that night, surely he wouldn't mess with a tramp like that.

I knew I had to get to the bottom of that phone call; but, I didn't know how. I decided to confront Keith next. I was mad at him for so many reasons. He didn't call to check on me while I was in Europe. He left the house in an awful mess, and why did he talk to someone from Ms. Jenkins' house.

I confronted Keith and he said exactly what any other man would say. Keith said, "I didn't get in until around 1:00 A.M. Saturday." "If someone called I wasn't home." I asked Keith about all the dirty dishes and that gross smell in our house. Keith said he had some of the guys over from the team, and they were all sweaty and dirty. He became a little sarcastic with me. He said that they would party somewhere else next time. If Keith had some guys over they must be having sex on the down low, because someone else besides Keith had been in our bedroom. I asked him about my down low theory, and he became very offended. Men on the down low consider themselves straight, but they have sex with other men. It goes on in a lot of communities.

Keith said, "You're thinking way outside the box Star." He said that he would never dream of having sex with another man, but one night we were playing with a sex toy, and Keith asked me to put it in his rectum. He tried to play it off by saying that he just wanted to try something new, but he left me puzzled. Maybe I'm wrong about Keith being on the down low, but something is going on. I just don't know what it is.

I also confronted Keith about not calling me while I was in Europe, and that fool smarted off again. This time he said, " I'm sick and tired of all these disappointments." "I am tired of the process of waiting for your body to heal." " And I am tired of you being a nagging wife." I said, "Hold up Keith." "I am doing all this for us." "And what do you mean by saying your tired of waiting for my body heal?" " You only last two minutes anyway." Keith had never talked to me like that before. I was totally shocked.

I asked Keith if we could cuddle and watch television, and he said, "No Star you need to get off your ass sometimes and do some work." I had to defend myself. I said, " I've just had surgery Keith." " Are you retarded or just plain foolish?" Keith said, " Neither of the above." I was getting ready to confront him about my bedroom sheets, but the doorbell rang. It was Elizabeth." She was wearing a sheer, black, gown and It was the middle of the day.

I said, "May I help you." Elizabeth said, "I came over to see if I could borrow some sugar." I said, "Look here Elizabeth." "If you ever come to my house again, you are going to regret it." Then I slammed the door in her face. I turned and cut my eyes at Keith, and then I said, "Keith if I ever catch you eyeing another whore, I will gouge your eyeballs completely out." Keith stormed out of the house, and he left there walking. I knew he was up to something, because we have a total of six cars. Keith has never walked anywhere since we've been married. He was turning into a total stranger.

Chapter 6

I started feeling very uneasy about myself. Keith had been acting strange lately, and our marriage was headed downhill. I didn't have anyone to talk to anymore, because Ms. Jenkins had stopped working out with me. I started having strange thoughts about Keith, then my thoughts turned into dreams.

I dreamt that Keith was seeing someone else. I woke up before I could determine if it was a woman or a man. I decided to find something else to do with my time. I started a needed organization in the community. It was called the B.W.C. That stands for the Black Wives Club. It was like a neighborhood watch; but, we weren't watching for criminals. We were watching out for sluts. We were sick and tired of Elizabeth and others like her who didn't have any respect for themselves or others. The B.W.C. was a club that consisted of three black women. One was myself, and the other two were stay at home moms. One of us was always watching out for the other women in the neighborhood.

There were thousands of accusations going around the neighborhood about Elizabeth. Our club found out that some of the accusations were true. The wives club found out that she was selling her body for $100.00 per hour. The rich men in our neighborhood were her best customers. We also found out that she was sleeping with men in exchange for high dollar gifts. She was into gifts like cars and jewelry.

The club had been organized for about two weeks, and then we caught Elizabeth coming from Donna Dillihunt's yard. Mr. Dillihunt was the only one home that night. His wife was at the hospital taking care of her father who had Lung Cancer. Elizabeth was only wearing a t-shirt and some panties when she came out of that woman's house. Elizabeth and Mr. Dillihunt were seen kissing and hugging all over each other in the front yard. Mr. Dillihunt was even groping her. They were doing all of this outside. One of the members in the club video taped the entire act. We deliberated on the matter, and we decided to send Mrs. Dillihunt an anonymous letter. The letter said the following:

Dear Mrs. Dillihunt,

A slut was seen coming from your home last night. There were several eyewitnesses who saw her too. Please educate your husband on sexually transmitted diseases, and tell him that God sees everything we do. Please watch the enclosed tape. God's got your back girl and so do we.

Signed,

The B.W.C

Elizabeth preys on men like Mr. Dillihunt. He's old, rich, and stupid. He's the C.E.O. of IBM computers in Chicago. He could be spending his money on starving people or sick kids, but he's investing his money in a whore. Mr. Dillihunt is in his early fifties. He probably doesn't know that there are some std's out there with new names. I wonder if he knows about Chlamydia, HPV, Trichomoniasis, and all that other nasty stuff. Mr. Dillihunt grew up in the time when all people worried about was Gonorrhea or the clap as some people called it. I hope Mrs. Dillihunt takes heed to the warning. Elizabeth had no business coming from her home. We have decided to put Elizabeth's name and address in the letter if we catch her coming from that lady's home again.

I finally saw Elizabeth advertising her body in one of Chicago's finest neighborhoods one night. She didn't see me, because my car was headed in the opposite direction. I pulled my car over to the side of the road and watched her for a minute. Elizabeth was advertising to a deacon who belonged to my church. I couldn't believe my eyes. I thought Mr. Allen was holier than thou, because he used to testify in church every Sunday. Mr. Allen talked to Elizabeth for about five minutes, and then he got out of the car with his pants unbuckled. His big, black gut was hanging over his pants. He moved over, and then I saw Elizabeth in the drivers seat.

I turned my car around and headed back in their direction. Mr. Allen's windows were fogged up too bad for me to see anything. I was devastated, because I was close to Mr. Allen's wife. They had four small children, and he was a well known doctor in Chicago. There is so much hidden sin that goes on behind close doors. Mr. Allen should have been ashamed of himself. Where was his wife and kids? I decided to talk to my preacher about Mr. Allen, because last week Mr. Allen prayed and asked God to remove all corrupt beings out of our community.

He called Elizabeth's name specifically. Mr. Allen was a hypocrite. He knew he was messing with that woman when he called her name last week. There should be a wives club in every single neighborhood, because there is an Elizabeth in every neighborhood. There is also an Elizabeth on every job. She even attends some churches. If you have friends or neighbors like her you don't need enemies.

Chapter 7

I haven't seen Elizabeth lurking in our neighborhood for a while. I heard that Donna had torn her butt up. The Dillihunts were a cacausian couple, but I heard that Mrs. Dillihunt could fight like a sister. Elizabeth was seen driving in the neighborhood from time to time. She was driving a black BMW. It was probably a gift that some fool had bought for her, because Elizabeth doesn't have a job. I don't consider prostitution as a career.

I decided to start working out again. It was March, and I wanted to look good for the summer. I worked out at the gym today for about two hours, and then I headed home. I was all sweaty and dirty. I went home and cut the shower on, but the doorbell rang before I could jump in the shower. I looked out of the window, and to my surprise it was Ms. Jenkins. I opened the door, and I said, "Hey Ms. Jenkins long time no see." She started yelling and screaming so bad, I couldn't understand her. She finally calmed down, and then she said, "Where in the hell is your husband?" I said, "What kind of business do you have with my husband?" Ms. Jenkins said that it was something awful. She said she hated to be the bearer of bad news, but she opened up her purse and pulled a pregnancy test out. The test was positive. She said that Keith had invited Elizabeth over one night, and Ms. Jenkins claimed that the two of them had sex. She said that her daughter had spent the night at my house. She said that was the only time that Elizabeth had stayed away from home all night.

Ms. Jenkins started talking about the time when I called her about her phone number being on my I. D. box. She said that Elizabeth was the one that called my house. She claimed that Keith had seen Elizabeth earlier that day, and he invited her over to the house to watch a late night movie. Ms. Jenkins said she didn't know Elizabeth had slept with him until she was late coming on her cycle. Ms. Jenkins said that she had just found out about her daughter's condition yesterday.

Ms. Jenkins claimed that Keith was aware of Elizabeth's condition. She said that Keith had been coming over to her apartment quite a bit. Ms. Jenkins said that he came by last week and handed Elizabeth the keys to a brand new Mercedes. Ms. Jenkins said that Keith told her it was a gift from the heart. She said she still didn't know that Elizabeth was pregnant.

I felt like kicking Ms. Jenkins' ass. I couldn't believe that exotic story, because Elizabeth was messing with every man in the community. I couldn't let Ms. Jenkins get away with a rumor like that. I felt as if they were trying to put a baby off on us, because they knew we had plenty of money. I ended up telling Ms. Jenkins about the Wives Club. I told Ms. Jenkins about the time we caught Elizabeth coming from Donna's home, but then Ms. Jenkins dropped the bomb on me. Ms. Jenkins said, "I took Elizabeth to the doctor today, and he said her EDC was January 4, 2003." My mouth dropped, and I went into total shock. The EDC is the estimated date of conception. I was in Europe on the exact same date. I started yelling and screaming. I couldn't believe my ears. Ms. Jenkins had dropped the bomb on me.

Ms. Jenkins was trying to console me, but I put Ms. Jenkins out of my house. Ms. Jenkins isn't part of the solution . She's part of the problem, because there's no way I would allow anybody living under my roof to carry themselves like a slut. Ms.

Jenkins left my house in tears. I started gagging immediately after she left. I had to go in the bathroom and throw up again. I started feeling as if Ms. Jenkins was telling the truth. I was so mad at Keith. I started ripping all his pictures off the wall. Ms. Jenkins had just brought the last piece to that puzzle I was trying to figure out. She also gave me the answer as to why Keith was acting so strange.

I knew I couldn't allow Keith and Elizabeth to get away with this. I was so angry at the two of them. I started to feel a lump in my throat. I was always dumb enough to believe that Keith was in love with me, but the light was finally shinning in my face. My mother use to say that Keith married me so he could have a housekeeper. She tried to stop me from marrying Keith, but I wouldn't listen.

My mother was angry at him, because he stood me up at the alter on our original wedding date. I was standing at the alter all pretty and pure, and Keith had skipped town. He left me standing at the alter looking like a fool. He didn't give me a honeymoon either . We went to Vegas, but Keith gambled the entire honeymoon. He lost $30,000 in one day. We didn't engage in sex at all. My mom stopped speaking to me after Keith and I married. She could see right through him.

Keith was in store for some revenge, and I am not talking about petty revenge either. I could tamper with his food or something, but that was too simple. Keith was in store for something like *Waiting to Exhale,* but his punishment was going to be a little bit worse. He knew I had longed to experience motherhood, but he chose to waste his sperm on a slut. The thought of Elizabeth having sex with my husband gave me goose bumps all over my body. I am not going to be able to survive this. I don't even want to kiss Keith anymore, because God knows what happened between those two.

Keith's team was playing at the Chicago Bulls Stadium tonight. I decided to confront Keith after the game. I had a gut feeling that Keith had been unfaithful, and I felt that our relationship couldn't be salvaged. I started to wait until he got home to confront him, but I am only human; therefore, I could not wait. I decided to go to the stadium and make myself known. I needed to talk to my husband in person, and I needed to talk to him right away.

Chapter 8

I got dressed and left the house around 4:00 P.M., because the game was going to start at 7:00 P.M. I was dressed to impress. I had on a black, denim dress that I had ordered from Chadwicks of Boston. I wanted to wear something comfortable, because I didn't know if I would have to kick Keith's ass.

I arrived at the stadium shortly, and Coach Matlock was sitting outside on a bench in front of the locker room. He tried to stop me from going in, but I pushed him out of the way and went right in. I spotted Keith, and I asked him to step outside. Keith started showing out in front of his other teammates. He said, " Did I tell you to come up here Star?" I didn't answer him, because I was steaming hot. The he said, "You better go home if you want some money this week." He also said, "You know you don't have a job, so you better stop while you're ahead." Then he said, "Don't mess with the hand that feeds you."

I stood there, and I looked at Keith for about two minutes without saying a word. I finally said, "Keith you just made the biggest mistake of your life." "I came up here to talk to you in private, but you chose to show out and act a fool in front of your team mates." "Your team mates won't be around to save you when you get home." Keith was still acting a fool. He laughed and said, " So what do you want me to do?" "Should I be scared?" Then I said, " If I were you I would be." Then I left the locker room. I didn't get to confront him about sleeping with

Elizabeth at all, because he was too much of a wuss to come outside.

I decided to stay and watch the game. I had something for Keith, but he didn't know it. I couldn't believe Keith tried to embarrass me by saying that he wouldn't give me any money. I could have went to school and had a nice career, but I loved Keith so much. I gave all of my hopes and dreams up for him. What an ungrateful bastard. I will never feel the same way about Keith again, but you know how the saying goes "Payback is a mother."

Chapter 9

I went to the concession stand and purchased some popcorn and a coke. The buttery smell of popcorn was all through out the air. The game was going great. Keith had scored twenty points, and it was close to half time. I decided to stay until half time, because I like to see the commercial breaks. The Chicago Bulls stadium delivers advertisements on a big screen message board. The first message was from Honda. The one after that was from Baskin and Robbins, and the last one was from me.

I paid a lady in marketing $300.00 to flash a message across the board for me. It said:

Smokin' Keith James can get a climax in one minute or less. The job is guaranteed. I hope you have a nice life.

Your wife, Star.

The stadium turned into a house of laughter. The commentators were laughing all over the place. One of the black commentators was chocking with laughter. He kept saying Smokin' Keith James. I could even see some of his closest friends laughing. Keith's mother was at the game, and she was so mad. She got up and left. She has never been fond of me anyway. She wanted Keith to marry one of the cheerleaders from high school, She said that I was too violent for Keith. I don't know why she said that, because I have only hit him a couple of times. I had a valid reason each time.

Keith was drowning in embarrassment. I could see it all in his face. He was trying to play it off, but he was down right embarrassed. Men hate for women to insult their manhood, and that's exactly what I did. I thought insulting Keith would make me feel better, but I was still very mad. I had all kind of thoughts running through my head. Did he sleep with that dirty slut in bed? Was he retarded enough to put our family at risk by having unprotected sex? Didn't he know I was going to put him through pure hell?'

I had all these thoughts running through my head at the same time. I was also thinking about 101 different ways to physically hurt Keith.

I had so many good things in mind until it was hard for me to narrow it down to just one. Something had obviously went to that fool's head. He had been acting like he was a prize lately. He had money, but he was far from being a prize. He could only last two minutes and that's all. I've seen dogs last longer than that. He's a good kisser and that's about it.

I can't believe he tried to show out like that with his dwarf of a penis. Keith's penis does not match his body. He's 6 feet 3 inches tall, but his penis is the size of an inch worm. I don't know why men try to reverse their attitudes on us, because we all have faults. Keith's fault is his penis. A real man can control his penis, but Keith's penis has a mind of it's own. I have to fake orgasms all the time, because Keith finishes before the hand goes all the way around on the clock.

Chapter 10

I had been home for a couple of hours. I didn't know what to do or who turn to. I didn't call my mother, because she would say I told you so. I didn't have any other local family members or friends that I would tell my business to. I had been with Keith all my life. I decided to stay just for tonight and try to talk to Keith.

Keith arrived home, and he had a blank look on his face. I said, "Keith let's talk." Then he said, "You made us lose the game." I tried to spare Keith. I tried to get revenge off my mind, but Keith started yelling at me as a matter of fact he started screaming.

He said the coach had suspended him from the team until further notice. I said, "Keith, I didn't make your team lose the game." " I wasn't out there playing." He said they lost, because a fight had taken place immediately after I left. He said I brought the devil in with me, and I forgot to take him back. He said the only thing he wanted to talk about was getting a divorce. He kept saying that he wanted a divorce over and over again. He even got the phone book out and started calling some twenty four hour emergency attorneys. I started to ignore Keith. I started tuning him out. I decided to drink some tea and call it a night. I put a kettle on the stove and boiled some water. My kettle was on for about twenty minutes, and then it started whistling. The kettle was whistling, and Keith was yelling at the same time. I was still ignoring him. I was so mad at myself for being married to a fool for such a long period of time. I had wasted so many valuable years of my life.

I had tuned Keith out, until I heard him pick up the phone and call Elizabeth right there in my house. He asked her when he could see her again. Then he said, "I'm still dreaming about that one night fling." Then he hung up the phone. I stood in the doorway looking at Keith's unfaithful behind. Keith said, "I was trying not to hurt you, but you pushed me Star." He said, "I am not always a two minute brother." " I lasted long enough to conceive a child to call my own with Elizabeth." I said, "Keith you must think I am some kind of a fool." "I told you earlier tonight that you were going to pay for the way you've treated me, and it's about that time." Keith said, " I am so sick and tired of all your threats." He said, "You're nothing but talk, and talk is cheap just like you." I asked him if he bought Elizabeth that car, and he got smart. He said, "It's my money, and I can do whatever I please with it." I got real mad at Keith, and I said "Keith you disloyal bastard." "You didn't have to unveil your relationship with Elizabeth like that." Keith said, "Stop hating on that woman." "At least she's out there working for what she wants."

Okay that did it. I was speechless. I ran in the bathroom, and I suddenly developed a mental block. I was so mad my head was spinning. The very last thing I can remember is calling Keith's name. Keith turned around and I sprayed his eyes for about three minutes with a can of mace. He was standing there yelling and screaming like a wuss. I kept on spraying and spraying and spraying. Next, I took a can of hair spray, and I sprayed it all over his uniform. Then, I took a match and set his clothes on fire.

Keith's clothes were on fire in less than two seconds. He couldn't take them off, because he couldn't see. I was still dwelling on the fact that Keith had slept with a slut. I didn't appreciate his messed up attitude either.

Keith managed to put the fire out of his clothes; but, he was struggling a great deal to get to the phone. He was still blinded by all the mace. He had big, blistered burns all over his dirty body. He had the phone in his hand, but I knocked it down. And, I snatched the plug out of the wall. Keith was yelling for help. I was still mad at him. I didn't have any remorse for that bum at all. I went in the bedroom and grabbed my purse, because I knew that someone would eventually hear all of the noise and call the police. I ran outside and jumped in my Escalade.

I didn't feel like going anywhere, because Keith had upset me so bad. I decided to go back in the house, but I went in without getting out of my vehicle. Yes, I drove my Escalade straight through the house, and I hit Keith instantly.

Keith was pinned between the wall and the front of the truck. Keith said, "Star your day is coming, You better hope I die." I opened the door of the Escalade and got out. I didn't try to move it. Our house had turned into a crime scene. Keith was still alive, but he was going into shock.

I exited the house through the garage. I needed some fresh air. Everyone was standing outside looking. I turned around and looked at everyone and said, "My husband slept with a whore and then tried to rub it in my face." A few women said you go girl. I started fumbling through my purse to see if I had the keys to another vehicle. I finally found the keys to my Navigator. I put the keys in the ignition and started to back out. There were a few guys who tried to block me in, and I said, "Move out the way before I hit you."

I sped off real fast. I didn't know where I was going, but I was going anywhere but here. I looked down in my purse to get my compact out, and then I heard a loud noise. I had hit something. I thought it was a dog, because I didn't see anybody walking. I jumped out of the car real fast, and it was Elizabeth. She was lying on the ground in some black, lace pajamas, and she was pregnant and all covered with blood. There was blood all over the hood of my Escalade. I panicked. I couldn't say anything more than Father forgive me for my hidden and my visible sins. It was truly a mistake. Elizabeth was just at the wrong place at the wrong time. I was shaking so bad. I couldn't do anything but sit on top of my vehicle and pray, and then Elizabeth said, "Help me please." I couldn't help her. I just couldn't. I said, "Did you sleep with my husband whore?" Elizabeth closed her eyes. I didn't know if she was alive or dead. I didn't touch her.

Today was a day within a day. I should have stayed in bed this morning. I had no idea that all this drama would occur. Keith is going to kill me if he lives. If he dies, then I will have to deal with God. I am going to have to deal with god either way it goes, because the lord said vengeance is mine. It belongs to him and not us.

The police, fire department, ambulance, and helicopters arrived. Keith and Elizabeth were both alive, but they were in critical condition. They both had to be airlifted to one of the local hospitals. Keith was going into shock, and Elizabeth was loosing a lot of blood. The emergency workers said Keith needed to pray for a miracle.

I was escorted to jail by the Brooks County Police Department. The officers advised me to remain silent, because there were a bunch of charges hanging over my head. They advised me to call an attorney as soon as possible. This was a test in my marriage, and I failed it. I should have let the lord have his way with Keith and Elizabeth. I started crying, because I knew that jail would be my home for a while. I intended to hurt Keith, but Elizabeth was an accident. Her black pajamas affected my ability to see.

I bet Keith learned a lesson from all this. If you love someone powerful enough you will snap if they don't love you back. Men are the cause of insanity for a lot of women. A bunch of women are mental hospitals, because a man put them there. The man who put them there is sometimes there father, boyfriend, or husband.

A man can damage a woman's mind for life. If she lets him, and that's what happened to me. I was determined to make Keith love me, but we're unequally yoked. Keith married me, because he liked the way I cooked and cleaned. He didn't love me as a person though. I married Keith because I knew he could play ball, and I knew he would hit it big one day.

Chapter II

Chicago jails are overcrowded. I had to stay in a holding cell all night. My booking took place this morning, and I was placed in a jail cell with five other women. I was charged with arson, failure to maintain a safe look out, striking a pedestrian, disorderly conduct and attempted murder.

I felt like a criminal, because I had to take a picture holding a board in my hand. The board had my first and last name on it. I was also assigned a number. I was no longer Star James. I became number 19528. Jail is a freaking nightmare. It stinks. The food sucks, and there's a lot that goes on that people just don't know about; for instance, one of the ladies in my cell tried to commit suicide this morning.

She cut her throat with some utensils she took from the cafeteria. She had been charged for hurting her husband too; but, he didn't pull through. He died from being bludgeoned to death. Two of the other ladies in my cell were lesbians. They kept me up all night, because they were performing various sexual acts. The other two ladies were in jail for prostitution. I often think about hurting them while their sleeping. It's real hard for me to share a cell with prostitutes. They are just so nasty.

I knew I would have to find a hobby in order to survive in here. Think about all the bad things that happen in the world. When it's put to an end, a lot of it ends up here. Jail is like being in hell on Earth. It houses people from all walks of life. It houses people of all different ages, and it's opened to anyone who messes up in life. Jail is just like being in a world inside of a world.

Chapter 12

I woke up this morning feeling febrile again. I told one of the jailers, and he passed it on to the jail's medical staff. I was hot, but I was sweating a cold sweat. I had a temperature of 104.5 degrees. I was rushed to the hospital, and the doctor said that my white blood counts were real low. He said that was a sign of serious infection.

The doctor took some blood cultures, and he determined that my body had set up a serious infection. He asked me if I had undergone surgery recently, and I told him I had recently undergone surgery two months ago. The doctor on call said that I needed a Hysterectomy like yesterday. I was handcuffed to a hospital bed, and I was ordered to remain there until further notice.

I started feeling depressed again, because I was dealing with this by myself. I started to miss my home life. I decided to pray this time and trust in God, because I was too weak to handle this all by myself. I didn't consult God before I had any of my surgeries. Keith was the only person that I had talked too, and he was the wrong person.

The doctor came back in my hospital room a few hours later. There were several other medical residents accompanying him. He said, "Ms. James your condition is far worse than I thought." "You will have to have a hysterectomy today or you could die." I said, "Explain the source of the infection to me." "I had surgery two months ago." "Did the infection occur because of the surgery?" I also asked him how the infection turned into something so fatal.

The doctor shook his head and said, "I hope you can handle this." "Your infection is caused by a venereal disease that was left untreated." I said, "What kind of venereal disease." He said that it was Gonorrhea. The doctor wasn't concerned with how I got it. He was just worried about saving my life. I said, "A who that was left un what?" The doctor said, "An emergency surgery today would be a life saving surgery for me." The frustration had started all over again.

I had to have an emergency surgery. The anesthesiologist put me to sleep, and the doctors went straight to work. The surgery lasted for about four hours, and then I had to be transferred to the Critical Care Unit on the first floor afterwards. My white blood count was only two hundred. Normal people have a white blood count of at least 10,000.

No one was allowed to come in my room without a mask, a hospital gown, and gloves. Our bodies don't have any defense against infections when the white blood counts are low.

I am thirty years old, and now my womb is gone . My body felt like crap, and depression was starting to sink in again. I started thinking about how I would never be able to experience the joys of motherhood. I couldn't believe that Keith had done so many low down things to me. I'm glad I'm not God, because if I was I would strike Keith down immediately.

My mouth started to become dry, and I felt feverish again. I was in a great deal of pain. I was sore from the waist down. I pushed the red nurses button, and I asked for some pain medicine. The nurse said that I couldn't have anything but ice chips for the next twenty four hours. It took her forever and a day to bring my pain medicine in. People treat you different when you're an inmate. The doctor came in and said you are real lucky to be a live. He advised me to use protection in the future. I told him that I contracted the venereal disease from my husband,

and he said, "I am a so glad we caught it in time." The doctor had totally changed his attitude when he found out the true story. Men always try to stick together.

I stayed in the hospital for three weeks, and then I was discharged. I was on my way back to jail. The jailer took me through back exits in the hospital, because inmates are not allowed to go out of the front entrance. We exited the hospital on the ground level, and there was a police car waiting to escort me back to jail.

Chapter 13

Today had to go down as one of the coldest spring days in Chicago. I cried as I entered the jail in a wheelchair, because I knew I was on my way back to another world. I cried even more and more as I walked through the jail's glass doors. I felt like asking God to open up the world and let me out. The jailer took me through security, and then we went back into the inmate area. The sound of the buzzing doors were sticking in my head. Some of the inmates were cheering me on, but I didn't know why.

One of the white female inmates handed me a newspaper. I opened it up and Keith's picture was on the front page. The article said that he was allegedly run over by his wife, and it said that he suffered third degree burns. It said that he was scheduled to have surgery later in the week. The doctors wanted to see if they could do a skin graft to promote the healing of some of his burns. I was near the end of the article, and then I looked up and saw a familiar face. It was my preacher. His name is Reverend Jackson.

Reverend Jackson was standing in front of my cell, and he was wearing a black suit. He had a bible in one hand and a newspaper in the other. He was allowed in the inmate area, because he is an ordained minister. My preacher started talking to me, and he wanted to know why I had let the devil cheat me so bad. I said, "Reverend Jackson my husband used to be perfect, and then he turned corrupt." "I didn't let the devil cheat me." "My husband cheated me."

Reverend Jackson said, "I have one piece of sound advice for anyone involved in relationships." "Don't ever try to establish a perfect relationship." "Relationships can't be perfect." "Man can't be perfect. God didn't put any of us on Earth to be perfect.""If you think you can establish a perfect relationship you're wrong." "There's only one man you can establish a perfect relationship with, and he will never let you down." "His name is God, and don't you ever forget it." I cried my eyes out, and then I gave my life back to God. It was a moment that would have given you chills. Our cell turned into a spirit filled placed. The two lesbians were even crying. God can bring his spirit into any place, and that's exactly what happened today.

I was waiting on the church choir to start singing, because Reverend Jackson had turned this jail around. We always expect perfection out of relationships, but we're asking for way too much. Keith was never perfect, and neither was I. We invest a lot of time in relationships and other worldly things, but we're wasting our time.

I started to let go of that negative bag, and I stopped feeling sorry for myself. I was in a terrible situation; but, there's always someone else who is worse off than you. I know I'm in a terrible situation; but, I can't do anything about that. God is the only one that can change things for a person. He's the only one I know that will take on your problems when they get too heavy to bear. I have already given my life back to him, because my load was just too heavy for me to carry by myself.

I've been through more in a couple of weeks than some people have been through in their whole lifetime. The devil is busy, but I have a weapon for him. I am going to use my spiritual warfare. I decided not to be oppressed by my circumstances. The devil has no place in my life. I am going to let go and let God. He's the only person I can depend on right now.

Chapter 14

You haven't felt heat until you've worked in a jail house cafeteria. It's like working inside of an oven or something. Jails don't hire people for jobs like cooking and housekeeping. These jobs are assigned to inmates.

The kitchen supervisor doesn't care what kind of condition your in either. My surgery is only six weeks old, and I still have to cook meals in an extremely hot kitchen . The kitchen is about the size of a closet., and there's always an inmate who comes in looking for trouble. Today, a female inmate came in and asked me to give her some extra potatoes and gravy. I said no, and then she tried to start a fight. Misery loves company. She's in here for life. She's the lady that bludgeoned her husband to death. The guards retained her quickly ; therefore, it didn't escalate to anything. I have noticed that some people give up in this place. They feel that they don't have anything to look forward to, but I know I have something to look forward to.

I have been through all these trials and tribulations, and I am still standing strong. I can't let go of the rope. I just can't. Yesterday, an inmate asked me what I could possibly have to look forward to, and all I could say is Jesus, Jesus, just Jesus! Jesus didn't get me into this mess, but I know he can get me out of it. Faith is the only thing that keeps me standing. Jail is a lot like every day life. Only the strong survive.

Chapter 15

Lights on! That's what the guard said this morning. Today is Saturday, and I don't have cafeteria duty. I washed my face and brushed my teeth, and then one of the guards started doing mail call.

I received a letter today. It was addressed to me, but there wasn't a return address or phone number on the outside of the envelope. The letter was from a man, as a matter of fact it was my first letter from a man. The man said that he had been involved in a situation similar to mine. He had been seriously hurt by a woman, and she left him with absolutely nothing. He was writing to me from a homeless shelter, because he had to start all over again. He included a phone number, and he asked me to call him when I had a chance. He also included a $25.00 calling card in the letter. He didn't give me his real name. He called himself Mr. Do Right.

We are allowed to make one phone call per day, so I decided to call Mr. Do Right shortly after breakfast. I didn't tell any of the ladies about him, because they are just like the women on the street. If they find out you have a good thing going, they will try to mess it up.

I stood in line for an entire hour. I was in a hurry to use the phone. We only have 15 minutes to use the phone, and some of the women try to sneak and go over. The lady in front of me stayed on the phone for 30 minutes. I politely asked her to get off the phone, and she called me a bad word.

I finally got my hands on the phone, and I called him. I called the Lighthouse Homeless Shelter, and I said, "May I speak to Mr. Do Right." The lady on the other end said," You have the wrong number." She was getting ready to hang up, but then she said, " Hold on I know Do Right, He came in last week." A gentleman came to the phone, and he said, "Do Right at your service." I was speechless, because his voice was so deep. It made my whole body tingle. I said, "Hi my name is Star." He replied by saying, "A beautiful name for a beautiful young woman.." I said, "I beg your pardon." He said that he had seen my picture in the local paper, and he said that he had fallen in love with my honey, colored eyes.

I decided to talk to him until someone started bitchin' about the phone. We talked for thirty minutes. I asked him if he would reveal his real name. He said, " Call me when you find out your court date, and I will make myself known then." I made a promise to call him, and inform him of my court date. If he looks as good as he sounds, then he's a knock out. This man could probably make you have an orgasms just by talking to you.

I went back to my cell, and I decided to start writing a journal. My first entry was about Mr. Do Right. His voice had seduced me over the phone. We didn't talk about anything sexual, but his voice had a sexual ring to it.

I also wrote about myself. I was becoming stronger and stronger each day. I started to feel a certain happiness again, because I had something else to look forward to. I picked up Mr. Do Right's letter again. I wanted to read it one more time. I took the letter out, and I shook the envelope. Something extra fell out.

My toes curled up when I saw it. It was a picture of Mr. Do Right. He was honestly one of the finest brothers that I have ever laid my eyes on.

SCANDALOUS CONFESSIONS

Keith's Confession

I know I have been a low down, dirty, low life to Star, but I never intended to hurt her. My father use to treat my mother the same way. He commanded her to do things, and she did them. He wasn't being low down, because he put a roof over our heads and, and we didn't want for anything.

Sleeping with Elizabeth was the worst thing that I could have ever done; but, she seduced me. She came over to my house while my wife was gone wearing nothing but a red, lace night gown, and then she started rubbing on my manhood. She pulled up her gown, and she had on some black crotchless panties. Elizabeth stood there with her almond, colored body. Her long, black curly hair covered the nipples on her breast. She tempted me so hard. I didn't know what else to do. She made me feel better than any woman had ever made me feel before. She is the only woman that has ever turned her naked body all the way around on my manhood. We rolled around in my bed for hours. I caressed her body as she gently moved up and down on my manhood. She has the greatest sex in the world.

Star and I will never get back together again, because the sky is the limit for her. She's gone off on the deep end. I wish I could relive the day I cheated again, and I would have put Elizabeth out of my house. I wouldn't have engaged in a sexual act with her. I believe in God's commandments. I wish I had of been strong enough to follow them.

Star left me in a terrible mess. I can't even stand to look at myself in the mirror anymore. I can't even stand up by myself. I regret marrying Star, because she's a hidden lunatic. I hope I regain my strength.

I am paralyzed from the waist down right now. The doctors are not sure if I will ever be able to walk again. Only time will tell. I am totally bed confined right now. Elizabeth is in a state of shock, and she is still fighting for her life. Be sure to pick up the sequel to this book to find out if the lord gets all of us out of this mess.

A Word from Star

Keith, Thank you for the ride no where. I wasted twelve years of my life with you. You told me you wanted a stay at home wife, and I gave you exactly what you asked for. The world is nothing but a playground to you. I still can't believe you unveiled your affair with Elizabeth in such a tacky manner.

You have already felt my vengeful anger, but that's nothing compared to what God has in store for you. I thought our relationship stood for something. I meant what I said when I stood before the alter, but what about you? Elizabeth is still young. She's still wet behind her ears. I am trying to think of a word to call you right now, but there isn't one. You had sex with someone who does it for a living. What does that say about you? The best things in life are free Keith, but remember you also get what you pay for. I hope you get exactly what you paid for, and I mean that with a passion.

<u>Elizabeth's Comments</u>
I don't think it's my time to die. I have only been in the world for nineteen years. There are so many things I haven't experienced yet. I can name a million places that I haven't seen. I would like to live to see old age, because I am still pregnant. My baby is going to need me.

I can't help it, because I'm gorgeous. Keith slept with me, because he had been casing me out for a long time. I don't love him. It was all about business for me. Keith is a VIP. I got thousands and thousands of dollars out of him. If Ms. James was satisfying him, then he wouldn't have to come to me. He's far from being a dog. He was very romantic with me. He lasted all night. We had sex until the wee hours in the morning, but I don't mix business and pleasure together. It's all about the Benjamins for me.

I hope I live to see my next birthday. I am planning on going to night school, so I can earn my GED. The doctor's said I have less than a fifty percent chance to live, but who knows. It's all in God's hands, and he does answer prayers that come from sinners too.

Questions About The Book

Q: How did you come up with the character Star?
A: She was derived from my imagination, but I developed some of her characteristics from people I associate with in my everyday life.

Q: Did you base your novel on any other book or books that are out on the market?
A: No. Somebody's Sleeping In My Bed has a combination of everyday life, religion, and complex situations. The various parts of the book have been creatively put together to form one unique novel.

Q: What inspired you to write this book?
A: My daughter inspired me to write the book. I supported her in fighting a battle against cancer and the process has made me a very strong person.

Q: What are you planning to do next?
A: I am currently working on the sequel to **Somebody's Sleeping In My Bed**. It is called Coming Home, and it will be available by the fall of 2004.

An Excerpt From Coming Home

A sneak preview at Coming Home
A small part from Chapter 1

Chapter 1

I got up this morning at 5:00 A.M., and fixed my hair real pretty. I tossed and turned all night last night, because I am going to go to court for my arraignment today. I 'm not sure if Mr. Do Right will make it, because he just started a new job this week.

My case has gained a lot of attention from the media, because there are a lot of women out there who feel that I didn't do anything wrong. I get thousands and thousands of letters each week from women who sympathize with me. I am hoping and praying that the judge will feel the same way. I have been in this place for two months now, and I am getting so sick and tired of looking at four dirty walls each day.

I am going to shout all over that court room, If the judge says I can go home today. I have one of the best attorneys around, so

I have faith that he can get me out of this mess. I am using an attorney that I found in the phone book. His name is Jerry Cochran. I hope he can persuade the judge to let me go home today.

I entered the courtroom, and my eyes were fixated on a familiar looking face. It was man, and his eyes became fixated on me too.

About the Author

Rosiland Crossland is a native of Memphis, Tennessee. She's married, and she has three children. She received a Bachelors Degree in Education, and she currently serves her community by teaching children. Her writing expertise has enabled her to enhance the minds of many children.

Crossland is currently working on her second novel. It is the sequel to *Somebody's Sleeping In My Bed*. Look for *Coming Home* in the fall of 2004. Someone does something in *Coming Home* that will totally blow your mind. You can purchase additional copies of this book at any bookstore that sells fine books.

Thanks for your patronage

0-595-30216-5

Printed in the United States
15658LVS00002B/583-594